Disneynature
AFRICAN CATS

SITA THE CHEETAH

By Laura Driscoll
Photographs by Keith Scholey, Marguerite Smits van Oyen,
David Breed, Natasha Breed, and Owen Newman

Special thanks to Keith Scholey
Printed in the United States of America
First Edition
1 3 5 7 9 10 8 6 4 2
Library of Congress Catalog Card Number on file.
ISBN 978-1-4231-4216-4
For more Disney Press fun, visit www.disneybooks.com

DISNEY PRESS
New York

In Africa,
a cheetah lies
in the tall grass.

Her tan fur and dark spots
help her stay hidden.
And right now,
that is a very good thing.

The cheetah, called Sita,
is not alone.
She has just had babies.

Keeping them hidden
means keeping them safe.

In the wild,
most cheetahs have
three to six cubs at once.
Sita has five cubs.

They drink her milk.

They stay close to her.

For now,

Sita is all they need.

But Sita must hunt
for herself and the cubs.
Sita hopes other animals
do not see her cubs.

Luckily, the cubs stay safe.
At six weeks old,
they follow Sita everywhere.
They watch. They learn.

Sita sees a gazelle.

She gets down low.

She creeps closer.

She is stalking her prey.

Then, she uses her speed
to chase the gazelle down.
Cheetahs are the fastest
animals on land.

Sita and the cubs eat quickly.
Then they move on.

Nearby, bigger animals
are hungry, too.
Sita wants to be gone
by the time they come.

From Sita, the cubs learn
to fear male cheetahs.
Females live alone.
But many male cheetahs
live in small groups.

These three brothers
try to rule the area
and may not want
cubs around.

Sita does everything she can
to keep her cubs safe.
But one night,
two cubs disappear.

Sita calls again and again.
But the cubs do not come.

Sita leads the cubs
to a safer area.
Hyenas soon show up.
Sita attacks.

Then the male cheetahs
catch a wildebeest.
The hyenas will try
to steal it.

Sita and her cubs
are safe.
Then a huge lion appears!
He is bigger than Sita.

But when he runs at her,
she runs at him!
At the last moment,
Sita turns and outruns him.
The lion is tired and walks away.

Soon Sita's cubs are
more than a year old.
They practice their
hunting skills
as they play.

They hunt as a team.
Sometimes they chase
animals to tire them.

The cubs soon learn
that some animals
are off-limits—
like lion cubs.

When a mother lion sees them,
she charges.
The cheetahs race off,
just out of reach.

Before long,

the cheetah brothers are back.

They capture one of the cubs.

Sita must leave a cub behind

to save the others.

She and two cubs escape.
Sita leads them as far away
as she can.

All night long,
Sita's ears perk up
at every sound.
In the morning,
she scans the plain.

At last,

Sita hears a cry.

It is her cub!

She has found

her way to Sita.

Sita and the cubs
run to the third cub.
They jump and play.
They are so happy
to be together again!

They will not be together
for too much longer.
The cubs are getting older.
Soon they will leave.

And before long,
they may raise cubs, too.
For this, like everything else,
Sita has trained them well.